Society Killed the Cat

Mari Taylor

A Mere 10% of People With Eating Disorders

Receive Treatment. Here are six of their stories.

Printed in the United States of America

ISBN 978-1-941749-34-0

4-P Publishing
Chattanooga, TN 37411

If you want to connect with Mari, you can connect with her at:
Mari.taylor@comcast.net
www.maritaylor1.com

DEDICATION

*This book is dedicated to anyone who has ever felt as if they needed to hide behind society's standards of "perfection." I would like them to know that they are not alone, and that they **will** get through this.*

ABOUT THE AUTHOR

Most known for the content she creates on YouTube, Mari Taylor is the author of "society killed the cat" and "how (not) to get fired from your job." Taylor was born and raised in Tennessee and still lives there with get family, while in the pursuit of becoming a young writer, YouTuber, and astronomer. To see more of Mari Taylor, subscribe to her YouTube channel @Captain aMARIca.

CONTENTS

PART ONE: RED

"Mental pain is less dramatic than physical pain, but it is more common and also more hard to bear. The frequent attempt to conceal mental pain increases the burden: it is easier to say "My tooth is aching" than to say "My heart is broken."

—C.S Lewis

"Pain is the feeling. Suffering is the effect the pain inflicts. If one can endure pain, one can live without suffering. If one can withstand pain, one can withstand anything. If one can learn to control pain, one can learn to control oneself." —James Frey

CHAPTER 1: ARDEN

Arden, Sawyer!" I heard the voices of Evan, Margo, Clifford and Brent coming towards us deep in the woods. As I ran towards the faint silhouette of Sawyer, mud splashed on my jeans, ruining them.

"Sawyer!" I yelled. I knew she could not hear me over the sound of the heavy rain. I took in my surroundings, using the faint moonlight as my only source of light. "Sawyer!" I yelled once more.

That time she finally came to a halt. "Arden," I heard again in the distance. It was Evan.

As I began getting closer to her, I heard the sound of cars racing down the nearby highway. When I finally reached Sawyer, I found her hunched over the street's curb, clothes drenched.

"What are you doing here?" she asked flatly. I did not answer, but stared at her frail body.

"S-Sawyer, please come back inside," I said.

She turned to me, staring at me blankly. "I said, what the heck are you doing out here?" she repeated, this time firmly. She shivered, pulling her damp, coarse hair out of her eyes.

"I just want to talk," I said, lowering myself to sit on the ground next to her.

Her face softened. "I have absolutely nothing to say. You're wasting your time." She gazed at the cars on the highway with a slight smirk on her face.

"Arden! Sawyer!" The voices were closer now.

"Sawyer, are you okay?" I asked.

She sighed, "I'm fine, Arden."

"Sawyer-," my voice trailed off.

"You know, all my life I've wondered what it would be like to fly... To soar away from your problems as if they were nonexistent," she began. She stood up, never taking her eyes off the cars in the distance.

"Once, Evan broke up with me, and I realized something-" Her voice trailed off as she took a step towards to highway. I followed her, suddenly feeling tenser.

"What did you realize?" I asked.

She turned to me, eyes watering. "Angels fly, too."

6 months earlier

Close your eyes and imagine. Imagine you are sitting in a room with the person you hate most. The hatred is mutual. "You're ugly... fat... worthless... you'll never amount to anything," they say, just to put you down.

Imagine you are bound to that person for the rest of your days. Imagine that the person is you. The room is your mind. There is no escape from the unbearable thoughts. There is no escape from the thoughts that consume your mind every second of the day.

Welcome to my life, or the closest thing to hell, as I like to call it.

How did I get to this point? I should have known...I should have known that there was no such thing as perfection. I did not choose to have an eating disorder. It snuck up on me as a healthy diet and simply something to change my life for the better. However, like any drug, anorexia is deadly, but addictive at the same time.

As I lay in the cool damp grass with my friends, Evan and Margo, I sighed, looking at the grey, colorless sky. It was one of the only days they actually let the red bands go outside to the nearby field. On your first day at Memorial Hospital, the nurses gave you a colored band that described the healthiness of your weight - red being worst and violet being best.

"What do you miss most?" Evan asked. Margo tugged at her short dark blue locks that were cut into a bob.

"My family," she said, staring blankly into the empty sky. "I hardly get to see them anymore—not like they'd actually care." Her voice trailed off. "I miss my mum, my dad, and my brother."

Brother. Once upon a time, I was actually close to my older brother, Tyler. Nevertheless, like everyone I have gotten close to, he left me... erased me from his life as if I never existed. I remember the day he told me that he wanted nothing else to do with me. I have to live with that every day of my life. That boy who I used to talk to for hours about pointless things; that boy who was my best friend is gone. Moreover, I will never see him again.

"What about you, Arden?" Evan asked. Before I could answer, memories flashed before my eyes.

"I'm tired of your bullshit, Arden," Tyler spat out. His once hazel eyes that were filled with nothing but kindness were now hardened and emotionless.

"Tyler -," I began, but he cut me off.

"No,' he said firmly. "Do you not understand what you're doing to mum and dad? They can't handle watching you die slowly. You're breaking them inside."

Hot and salty tears ran down my face. "I'm sorry," I managed to get out.

"I don't have a little sister anymore," he said. "She left me a long time ago. Now I just have an eating disorder living down the hall."

I tried to say something... anything, but only uncontrollable sobs came out.

"At the rate you're going now, you will die soon. I don't want to stick around and watch that happen." He turned away from me, facing his bedroom door.

"Tyler, please," I begged. My voice was practically a whisper, barely audible over my faint cries. "I'M SORRY!" I yelled with all of the strength that I had left into the darkness of the night.

"Screw you, Arden." His voice was strong, but his voice trembled. His lips gave in, he let out a small cry as guilt, and sadness overwhelmed him. "All you've ever done is make life for mum and dad a living hell."

"Arden?" Evan asked.

I shivered. "I'm sorry, what was the question?" I asked with a weak smile.

"What do you miss most?" he repeated.

I shrugged. "I miss myself, which is something I lost a long time ago. I should be out living my last few years as a teen, not in an eating disorder unit. I miss my friends; I miss school; I miss my freedom; I miss black coffee; and I miss my family. We only get to live life once, and I'm wasting it."

I lifted my frail body off the ground and sighed heavily. "I'm going inside."

That night, more memories began to emerge:

Small drops of water attacked my body as I ran across the field and towards my home. Only five more minutes... five more minutes to run and then I can go back inside. Focusing on the road ahead of me, I sprinted a bit quicker. My shoes pounded heavily across the ground causing the mud to splash up my leg, and stain my new jeans. I took a deep breath, reminding myself that the more I exercised, the closer I got to my goal weight of 85 pounds. I looked around my surroundings; everything was suddenly fading to grey. I need to get moving, I told myself. I need to keep pushing. My muscles s began to tense, I felt like a ribbon slowly falling to the ground. I did not feel a hit; it felt like falling in a black hole, and now all I saw was darkness. I felt so alone.

"Arden!" I heard echoing. It was Tyler. His voice began to fade, as my vision dimmed into nothing but sheer darkness.

The next morning I woke up, panting. I had spent my whole night thinking of Tyler and his words to me. At the rate, you are going now you will die soon. I do not want to stick around and watch that happen.

As I lay down on the cool, uncomfortable hospital bed, I looked around the small room. The smell of the room was foreign - nothing like the scent of home. We will get home soon, I thought. We just need to pull ourselves together.

Shaking away my thoughts, I pulled myself out of the bed and walked towards the single window. I glanced out the rain-speckled pane, drinking in the sight of raindrops pounding against the pavement, only to be interrupted by a soft knock on my door. In came a nurse with a small clipboard wrapped in her arms.

"Good morning," she said in her honey-like voice. I gave a slight wave, still looking out of the window. "It's time for your weigh-in," she said. "Strip down and meet me down the hallway."

I nodded as she closed the door softly. I hated nothing more than the daily weigh-ins. The nurses and counselors told me countless times that the number that appeared was just a number, but it was so much than that. Each day I spent here, the further away I got from being thin - the further away I got from achieving perfection. I carefully took off my pale blue pajamas and folded them carefully, placing them on my bed.

I booted open the monochrome wooden door and slowly stepped into the corridor, shivering from the cold sensation on the bottoms of my feet.

"Step on the scale," a small, stout nurse said, yawning.

I wrinkled my nose at the stench from the hospital's hallways. I gazed at the other girls around me. They all could not be any more different; and yet I was probably twice the size of every single one of them. I used to have a body like that. I used to be thin. I took in a deep breath and stepped on the scale. The next several moments felt like hours.

"100 pounds," the nurse said as she scribbled something on her clipboard.

My heart nearly dropped…100 pounds of disgusting fat. A lump formed in my throat. I felt lugubrious. I wanted to crawl in a hole, or at least be in any other place than where I was now. Hanging my head, I stepped off the scale and walked back to my room.

Fat, lard, huge.

"Good morning," Margo said as she placed her tray of fresh food next to Evan's. Her short blue hair was pulled into a tight bun over her head. Bags burrowed under her hardened grey eyes. I set my tray across the rounded table from them. I do not need to eat. I do not need a muffin (500), I do not need yogurt (150), and I do not need an apple (50). My eyes darted around the room. There were no nurses looking yet. Carefully, I pushed the food into a napkin and put it into the trashcan.

"Good morning," I finally said.

"I'm so tired of this place," I added, addressing no one in particular after a few moments of silence. "I'm tired of life."

"Aren't we all?" Evan said with a small grin. Margo nodded as she slowly took a bite out of her bagel. She carefully looked around the room, brows furrowed.

"Arden, someone's going to notice that you aren't eating," she said in a hushed tone.

I practically rolled my eyes to the back of my head. "I don't care," I said. "They can tube me if they want." I must not eat. I must not eat.

I took her tray and pulled it towards me. Evan and Margo's eyes widened, shocked at my actions.

"We're better than this," I began. "It's not like the people here actually care about us. Their main objective is just to make us gain weight, and then send us away. Well, maybe I don't want to lose weight."

I do not have a little sister any more. She left me a long time ago. I just have an eating disorder living down the hall.

My voice trailed off. "When I was losing weight, I finally had control of something in my life. And that's something that I want to get back."

"Let's do it," Evan said. "We can take back control of our lives."

I must not eat. I must not eat. I must achieve perfection.

"Margo?" I asked. Her eyes fell to the floor.

At the rate you are going now, you will die soon. I do not want to stick around and watch that happen.

"I'm in," she said." We can take back control of our lives."

I must not eat. I must take back control of my life.

"You will lose someone you can't live without, and your heart will be badly broken, and the bad news is that you never completely get over the loss of your beloved. But this is also the good news. They live forever in your broken heart that does not seal back up. And you come through. It's like having a broken leg that never heals perfectly—that still hurts when the weather gets cold, but you learn to dance with the limp."

--Anne Lemont

CHAPTER 2: MARGO

Life with an eating disorder, if you can call it life, is similar to a puppet show. You are the dancing, smiling puppet, and your disorder is the puppeteer. It tells you when you are going to eat and how much. It even controls what you say. "I'm fine"... "I ate earlier"—all lies. At a certain point, you find yourself simply not caring about your health, nor whom you hurt in the process. Your whole life slowly becomes centered on reaching your next goal weight.

As for me, I do not remember exactly how it started. I went from restricting a few unhealthy foods to not eating for days at a time. So there you go, smiling as your bony body bounces around onstage. Some clap at your slenderness, while most stare in horror at what you have become. The puppeteer has taken all control of your life.

The funny thing is that only three years ago I wondered how people with depression and eating disorders ever got to that point. Ha!—but look at me now. I am exactly what I never understood as a 13 year old—depressed, suicidal, and diagnosed with anorexia nervosa. My struggle with anorexia went much deeper than just trying to the "perfect image." It was not just a "phase" or "a way to get attention." It was something that was a way to control my life. With all the hell my life has been recently, choosing to starve or reach my goal was something I actually could take control of in my life.

"So how have you been, Margo?" Mrs. Sue, my counselor asked me.

~~I am tired, hungry, afraid, depressed, broken, sad, lonely, hurt, upset, and angry at the world, worthless, lost, pathetic, bitter, and lifeless.~~

"I'm fine," I lied.

"I'm not stupid," Mrs. Sue said softly. "Tell me the truth."

I looked at her blankly. I clenched my fist, forcing myself not to do anything that I regretted. "I. Am. Fine," I said flatly.

"Margo—, "she began, but I cut her off.

"Look, I don't need this," I said. "I told you that I was fine. And I don't need some woman telling me exactly how I feel 24 hours a day."

She stared at me, eyes widened. "I've been at this job for over twenty years; I know when a patient is lying to me."

I clenched my teeth. "You don't know me," I spat. "You've not heard me scream at my nightmares every night - Never felt the battle scars on my thighs; never taken the chance to actually get to know me; never seen me at my lowest point. So I ask now, how the hell can you tell me how I am feeling."

Silence filled the room for a few moments. Each second seemed to go by slower than the last.

"I think that this session is over," I finally said as I left the room.

~~~

I found Arden and Evan sitting outside on the grass, staring at the clouds. I pulled myself down next to Arden and grunted.

"So how was your session?" Evan asked.

"I swear I hate that woman so freaking much," I seethed. My fists were still clenched from the meeting.

"So, not good?" Evan asked with a small smirk, blue eyes shining.

I let out a dry laugh, punching him lightly. "Have I ever told you how much you annoy me, Evan?"

He blew me a kiss, "It's a part of my charm," he said. "The ladies love it."

Arden nearly choked. "Sure thing, Evan," she said. "Keep telling yourself that. Nearly as an afterthought, "Gosh, I hate this place," she mumbled

"Want to go on a jog?" Evan suggested.

She nodded, messing up his curly dark hair. "I think that that's possibly the smartest thing that you've said all day."

"But what if we get caught?" I asked in a small voice.

"There's this moment in life where you don't worry about the 'what ifs' anymore... When you do not want to get better. You just don't care." She got up and Evan joined her. "You coming, Margo?"

~~I am afraid. My body already is worn out as it is. I just want rest.~~

"I'm in."

"The battle you are going through is not fueled by the words or actions of others; it is fueled by the mind that gives it importance."

—*Shannon L. Alder*

CHAPTER 3: SAWYER

Precisely a week after the first time I was admitted into Memorial Hospital, my mom finally decided to open her eyes and see that I had a problem. Whenever you think of someone living with an eating disorder, you usually think of someone that is experiencing depression, but in reality depression is an effect of dying...I guess I am dying.

Today was my first day of being readmitted into Memorial Hospital. It has been nearly a year since I have been an inpatient. The one thing I remember about my experience, of course, was that it was depressing as hell. Every afternoon everyone met in the hospital's bottom floor, sitting around a small pink carpet.

So here's how it went in the pink circle of death: About fifteen of us sat around the circle (most of us sitting so close that you could practically hear the faint heartbeat of the person sitting next to you) and listened to Amanda, the support group leader, ramble aimlessly about life; giving yet another "motivational" speech, and basically telling us if we don't shove food down our mouth, we die. Then we state our name, diagnosis, age, and how we are doing. I, as always, said the same thing:

Hi, my name is Sawyer Reynolds. I have been diagnosed with anorexia nervosa. I am fifteen years old. And other than the fact that I have been admitted into the nuthouse, I am just dandy.

Amanda would encourage us to share every aspect of our lives. It felt like hours would go by filled with people mentioning things as simple as their favorite color. During the meetings, I would usually sit by this girl named Arden. Although she was three years older than I was, we were fast friends. I wonder how she is doing, I thought. I guess I will find that out today.

When I arrived at the hospital, I received a red band around my right arm and was told to unpack my bags. After doing so, I went outside where the other red bands were. There I spotted a girl. Her hair was styled in tight ringlets around her face. The breeze blew through her curls, straightening them into waves that whipped about behind her. Arden.

"Arden!" I yelled with a beaming grin. She quickly turned around. Her jaw dropped as she saw me. I ran towards her, wrapping my arms around her. "Oh, my gosh," I heard her whisper.

I smiled, only to see two people following Arden. The boy stared at me suspiciously.

"If you're checking me out," I began. "I hope you are enjoying the view."

He laughed. "I'm Evan," he said. "And this is Margo." He motioned towards a petite girl with bright blue hair. She gave me a small wave.

"Welcome back to the nuthouse," Arden said with a small grin. "I've missed you."

~~~

Later that evening I wrote in my notebook the thin commandments:

1. If you are not thin you are not attractive.

2. Being thin is more important than being healthy.

3. You must buy clothes, style your hair, take laxatives, starve yourself, and do anything to make yourself look thinner.

4. Thou shall not eat without feeling guilty.

5. Thou shall not eat fattening food without punishing thyself afterwards.

6. Thou shall count calories and restrict intake accordingly.

7. What the scale says is the most important thing.

8. Losing weight is good/gaining weight is bad.

9. You can never be too thin.

10. Being thin and not eating are signs of true will power and success.

KNOCK, KNOCK, I heard at the door.

"Come in," I called, carefully putting my notebook under the pillow. It was Arden.

"Hey, Sawyer. I was wondering if you wanted to meet with Evan, Margo and I. We have a surprise for you."

I gave her a dry laugh. "Arden, are you kidding me? It's nearly curfew and we could get into serious trouble."

She snorted. "Relax, I'm your friend. I wouldn't get you into trouble on your first day."

I groaned. "You're lucky we're friends."

She flashed me a devious grin that stretched practically from ear to ear. "I'll be back in fifteen minutes. Wear something warm."

After Arden left, I slowly walked towards the dresser next to my bed. My eyes fell on the mirror hanging over it.

Fat, worthless, ugly, stupid, I heard a voice inside of me say.

I closed my eyes tightly, wanting nothing more than to shut the voices out. As usual, my attempts failed. They just kept talking... taunting me.

It's funny how I call the voice "they," while in reality, the voice was singular, and it was my own. I quickly brushed this off and pulled a grey hoodie out of my dresser.

Just look at yourself... you are disgusting.

As I slipped the hoodie on, I heard a knock at the door. It was Evan.

"Hey, Sawyer."

"Um, hey. I don't mean to sound rude in any way, but what are you doing here?"

Slowly, a rosy scarlet color spread over his cheeks, making his face take on an almost childlike appearance. Evan quickly turned his head away, embarrassed by his reaction.

"Um, Arden wanted me to bring you to our surprise." His eyes fell on me. He smiled, just a little smile at first, but as it grew, it pressed his rosy cheeks up and slowly revealed his teeth.

"Why are you smiling?"

"It's nothing."

"Why are you looking at me like that?"

"Because I enjoy looking at attractive people—you happen to be one."

I snorted. "I don't know if I should be flattered or really creeped out."

"It's okay, Sawyer, you don't have to deny—"

I cut him off. "Don't even finish that sentence. His chuckle was light, and laced with a hum of amusement at the matter.

"Gosh, you are something else," I mumbled. "We should get going."

He grinned. "Follow me."

~~~

Evan led me out to a balcony where Margo and Arden waited. The sun had completed its tour for the day, and had now been replaced by myriad stars, which dotted the inky canopy. A low, waning moon hovered tenuously in the twilight firmament, bestowing a very dim light upon the land. It was a cool, windy night; the swaying of trees and rustling of leaves could be heard but not seen, as the encompassing darkness had blotted out all but the faintest light. Briefly, a dark, wispy cloud eclipsed the crescent moon. I shivered.

"You cold?" Evan asked while raising an eyebrow.

I nodded. "Yeah, but I'll be fine. I'm a big girl."

He laughed. "Take my jacket."

"Thanks," I said as I slipped the jacket on. Several seconds of silence passed.

He dug around in his pocket for a minute before dragging out a cigarette and lighter. I raised an eyebrow as he lit it and took a long drag.

"I didn't know you smoked," I said as I crossed my arms. "How'd you even get that in here?"

He blew the cloud of smoke into my face, causing me to go into a coughing fit, and he smirked that crooked smile. "Want to try one?"

I shook my head. "I think I'll pass on that."

Margo and Arden walked over towards us. "I'll take one," Margo said. Evan handed her a cigarette and turned to me.

"Why do you do it?" I asked.

"Do what?" Evan said.

"Smoke."

"I do it for the rush, I guess. 'Makes me feel alive."

"You do realize smoking could kill you, right?" I asked.

He smirked. "To me, smoking represents all of the dangerous, yet beautiful things in life. I'd much rather be happy for a single moment—despite the fact that it could lead to my death—than live a life without excitement...without thrills."

"I never thought of it like that," I said. "I still think you're stupid, but that's very insightful—I'll give you that."

He laughed. "Has anyone ever told you that your eyes are beautiful? They remind me of Margo's hair."

I laughed suddenly and shortly. "My eyes are brown, you idiot."

Margo paused and lit her cigarette. She held it close to her body, avoiding eye contact from either of us. She giggled shortly and took a puff on her cigarette.

"Are you guys ready yet?" Arden asked.

Evan shook his head. "Yeah, let's go."

To my surprise, Arden pulled out several stones. She paused and handed me one. I felt the cool grey stone in my hands.

"Why did you give me this?"

"You'll see," she said as she handed Margo and Evan a stone as well.

"What are your fears?" Arden asked as she rested her hand on the railing of the balcony.

"Why?"

"In order to get out of the 'nuthouse' alive, you have to face your fears. The first step to doing so is admitting them."

"Sometimes, I'm afraid to be happy because every time I'm happy, something goes wrong. I always seem to screw things up. I'm a mess," I said. I took a slow breath. "It's stupid..."

"No, it's not," Margo said softly. "Our deepest fear is not that we are inadequate. Our deepest fear is that we are powerful beyond measure. It is our light, not our darkness that most frightens us. We ask ourselves, 'Who am I to be brilliant, gorgeous, talented, and fabulous?' Actually, who are you not to be? You are a child of God. You're playing small does not serve the world. There is nothing enlightened about shrinking so that other people won't feel insecure around you. We are all meant to shine, as children do. We were born to make manifest the glory of God that is within us. It's not just in some of us; it's in everyone. And as we let our own light shine, we unconsciously give other people permission to do the same. As we are liberated from our own fear, our presence automatically liberates others."

"Impressive," I said. "Where'd you get that?"

Margo smiled weakly, "Those are the words of Marianne Williamson. Read it in one of my books."

"Ahh, so you read?" Evan said. "How come you never told any of us?"

"I didn't think it mattered."

Arden continued. "Now throw the stone over the balcony, while yelling your fear."

Took in a deep breath. "I'm afraid of letting myself be happy," I yelled. I threw the stone and instantly felt a sense of relief.

I let out a loud yawn, extending my arms. "It's getting late," I said. "We should head back before its past curfew."

"The object of a New Year is not that we should have a new year. It is that we should have a new soul and a new nose; new feet, a new backbone, new ears, and new eyes. Unless a particular man made New Year resolutions, he would make no resolutions. Unless a man starts afresh about things, he will certainly do nothing effective."

—*G.K Chesterton*

CHAPTER 4: MARGO

Hello, Margo," Mrs. Sue said.

I grinned, trying my best to fake a smile. "Hello."

As my eyes slowly adjusted to the dim lights in the room, I noticed a few pictures of a young woman. She had rich dark brown hair that was cut neatly, stopping right above her shoulders.

"Is that you?" I asked.

She nodded. Near the middle of her office, I saw three large, red sofas forming a U letter with a rather low table in front of them. There was nothing on that table but a large vase with three beautiful red roses sticking out of it. I looked over my shoulder and spotted several photo frames all over the wall; pictures of family and friends, along with several framed awards and certificates. Swiveling my gaze to the other side, I spotted endless shelves coating the walls, filled with books. Many of these books were obviously special editions or collection items, and some looked at least a decade or so older than me.

Several lit candles were hung on the sides and their plates were covered with dried wax. At the desk, I saw several more large candles and smirked. I wondered how anyone could put a candle and a computer near the same area.

"So how are you, Margo?" she asked in her soft raspy voice.

Here we go again, I thought.

"Just grand," I said.

She chuckled softly. "You know, you remind me a lot of myself when I was your age. Growing up for me was difficult. Being raised by my aunt - she did a lot of things to cope with pain. This included dieting. One week it was this diet, the next it was another. I grew up with the assumption that I am not supposed to be happy with my body.

Once I hit high school, I began restricting, and even tried to get myself to purge whatever I did eat. Bulimia took over and I became sickly. This ruined the relationships I had with friends and family.

It was not until I hit rock bottom when I knew I needed help. I realized that I was not happy with where I was. I wanted to actually have relationships that were functional...I wanted to live a day without lying to someone or faking a smile. I realized bulimia had taken over my whole life and 'it' became so controlling that my whole life centered on dropping the next few pounds. Friends that I once talked to for years were now cut out of my life completely.

Almost two years later, I decided to turn to recovery. I was tired of destroying my life. It was a wakeup call. I kicked my butt in gear and I was ready to fight this. I was no longer going to let this destroy me. Recovery was hard. Hell, it felt like it was impossible. But once I did so, I took back my life. And I'm about to help you take back your life."

My face flushed ghostly white as my jaw dropped. "You never told—"

She cut me off. "You never asked." As I stared at her in awe, she pulled out a small leather notebook and extended it towards me. "So I hear you like to read."

I nodded, placing the small notebook in my lap.

"Have you ever thought about writing?"

"Actually, no," I said as I felt the rugged texture of the notebook in my palms.

"What are your passions, Margo?"

"Reading," I said with a small smile. "When reading, you enter the world of an author... a world that was crafted just from their imagination. It's the closest thing to magic that we have."

"Maybe writing is something that you can try. Channeling your energy into something positive can help you towards recovery."

Arden's voice rang in my head:

We are better than this. It is not as if the people here actually care about us. Their main objective is just to make us gain weight, and then send us away.

"Okay," I said with a weak smile. "I'll try it."

~~~

Later that day I met Arden, Sawyer and Evan in the field out back.

"So how was it?" Evan asked.

"Actually, not that bad," I said with a weak smile.

"We were going to head out for a jog," Arden began. "Would you like to go?"

Maybe writing is something that you can try. Channeling your energy on something positive can help you towards recovery. Recovery was hard. Hell, it felt like it was impossible, but once I did so, I took back my life. And I'm about to help you take back your life.

"No," I said. "I think I'll just stay here."

"Okay," Arden said. "We'll see you at support group today."

~~~

Arden, followed by Sawyer and Evan, walked into my room nearly five days after my second session and sat by me on the edge of my bed.

I looked up at them once, and then continued scribbling in my journal. Arden glanced at it, raising an eyebrow.

"What are you writing?"

"Nothing yet," I began. "You see, my brain decided to be a jerk today and now I can't think of anything."

"Write about us," Sawyer said with a beaming smile. "Of course, I would be the main character."

I laughed. "Sure thing, Sawyer."

"We were about to go for a jog," Arden offered. "You coming?"

Recovery was hard. Hell, it felt like it was impossible, but once I did so, I took back my life. And I am about to help you take back your life.

"Nah, I'll just stay here."

"But you made a deal," Arden said flatly, empty of emotion. Then I remembered what Arden told me much earlier:

We are better than this. It is not as if the people here actually care about us. Their main objective is just to make us gain weight, and then send us away. Well, maybe I do not want to lose weight.

"You said that while we were here, we would lose weight together."

~~Well, maybe I do not want to lose the weight now. Maybe I want to recover.~~

"I'm sorry," I said. "I just want to stay in here." Evan and Sawyer looked at me in awe.

"We made a deal, Margo," Arden said calmly. "Does that mean anything to you?"

My face flushed red. "Arden, I came here to get better, not go further into my eating disorder. This may seem crazy, but I'm tired of being under- weight," my voice broke. "I miss my friends, my family, and my innocence. And you're taking away my chance of getting that back."

Her normally calm and pleasant demeanor slowly changed as her face contorted in an all-consuming anger; her nostrils were flaring, her eyes flashing and closing into slits; her mouth was quivering and drooling, slurring words that were unintelligible came spewing into space like a volcano releasing its pent-up emotions into the darkness. Her hands closed into fists and she crouched forward, daring me to deny her one more time.

I looked past her at the other two. "Sawyer, Evan—you deserve better than this.

"Fine," Arden said as calmly as she could. "Stay here for all I care."

~~~

Dear journal, it has been three weeks since I last talked with Arden, Sawyer and Evan, and since then, my life... and weight has seemed to change for the better. I have actually made it to 105 lbs. Mrs. Sue says that with the progress that I am making now, I might be able to go home soon. I even moved up from a red band to a yellow band. While in yellow band, I met this girl named "Clifford," but her name is really Briar. And she is hilarious. Clifford always seems to make me laugh at the weirdest of times. Clifford got her nickname because a couple of weeks back, she tried highlighting her once bright blonde hair pink. Long story short, the highlights ended up being the wrong color and turned her hair bright red. Ever since then, every inpatient (including some nurses) called her Clifford.

Later that day, I found Clifford sitting in her usual spot in the cafeteria with Brent, another inpatient. I walked up to their table and placed my tray next to Brent's.

"Hey," I said with a slight wave. The three of us mostly spoke of random things. Our conversations could range from talking about how boring the nuthouse was, or what we would do once we got out. The great thing about

Clifford is that she never seemed to run out of things to say, and always seemed to beam of happiness. Sometimes it was hard to believe that she even had an eating disorder.

Brent once told me during dinner that they were going to head over to a friend's house later to hang out. One of the freedoms you got as a yellow band is the freedom to leave the facility grounds during free time, as long as you were back by curfew. Then, he asked me if I wanted to go with him and Clifford. Of course, I said yes, because I was not really in a position to pass up on friends.

We got to the house where Clifford and Brent's friends were. Brent knocked on the door and a short, stout girl with dark brown hair answered the door. As the door opened, the girl hugged both Brent and Clifford.

"This is our friend Margo," Clifford said with a smile.

"I'm Erin," the girl said as she waved at me.

Everyone was in the living room of the house. The room was quite smoky, and loud music blasted inside. Clifford and I sat in a circle with several other kids who looked much older than me. We talked for what felt like hours. I even met this cool person named Aidan who refused to ever cut his hair...Clifford would joke and call him Rapunzel instead of Aidan. We laughed when she said that. I do not really remember everything we talked about, but somehow I ended up with a new group of friends and quite the story to write about in my journal.

Take Care, Margo

"I am forever engaged in a silent battle in my head over whether or not to lift the fork to my mouth, and when I talk myself into doing so, I taste only shame. I have an eating disorder."

—*Jenna Morrow*

CHAPTER 5: ARDEN

I must not eat. I will not eat. I cannot eat. I must not eat. I will not eat. I cannot eat. I must not eat. I will not eat. I cannot eat. I must not eat. I will not eat. I cannot eat. I must not eat. I will not eat. I cannot eat. I must not eat. I will not eat. I cannot eat. I must not eat. I will not eat. I cannot eat. I must not eat. I will not eat. I cannot eat. I must not eat. I will not eat. I cannot eat. I must not eat. I will not eat.

I must not eat. I cannot eat. I must not eat. I will not eat. I cannot eat. I must not eat. I will not eat.

I must not eat.

"Love never dies a natural death. It dies because we do not know how to replenish its source. It dies of blindness, errors, and betrayals. It dies of illness and wounds; it dies of weariness, of witherings, of tarnishings."

—Anias Nin

CHAPTER 6: SAWYER

There have always been voices in my head, telling me that I am not good enough, but today for me was particularly a bad one. I sat in the darkness of the night, shaking. I can get through this. I do not have to listen to the voices. I bled the salt of my soul and it poured from my eyes against which my clenched fists pressed, blocking all of the light. I saw the darkness that I knew would soon swallow me and I feared it, longed for it.

I heard a soft knock at the door and quickly wiped my tears away. It was Evan. I looked at my eyes, and then stopped. He did not say anything, and he did not need to. One look in my eyes told him everything. He was one of the only people who could see right through me as if I were glass.

"Evan—" I began, but he cut me off by wrapping his arms around me tightly.

"What's wrong?" he asked softly. "You can tell me."

I burrowed my face in the crook of his neck, letting only a few tears stream down my cheeks. I used to do so well in school, but now that I have been staying here, my grades have been falling by the second, I thought. The people that I call friends, turned out actually not being my friends. I constantly feel alone. I am worthless. I just want to fall asleep one day and never wake up.

"It's nothing," I said. "I'm fine. But what are you doing here, anyways?"

"I just came to check on you." His brows furrowed as he tightened his grip around me.

Do you ever get that feeling where you just do not want to talk to anyone? You do not want to smile or fake being happy, but at the same time, you do not really know what exactly is wrong with you. You start to feel more comforted when you are alone, rather than with some people. You feel as if that when you are alone there aren't people bombarding you with questions such as "are you okay?" or "how are you?" even when they wouldn't take "I don't know" for an answer. Yeah, this is that feeling. I turned my face away from his, hiding the tears that ran down my face.

"Sawyer," Evan began. "You know you can trust me. You can tell me anything."

I cut him off. "That's the thing, Evan. I cannot trust anyone. Anyone I ever let get close to me, ends up leaving me. I trusted Arden, but she ended up only pushing me further downhill with my eating disorder...I trusted Margo, but she ended up leaving me behind. And I trusted you—"

"Sawyer, you can trust me," he said softly. He looked me right in the eyes.

"I don't think I can go on anymore," I said, my voice breaking. "I want to recover, I really do, but the voices always convince me that getting to my next goal weight is more important than saving my life. I feel dead inside... Like a living corpse."

Both of us were sitting in the corner of my dully lit room, the windows almost bursting at the seams with the now radiant morning sun. A nostalgic feeling had indulged itself onto both of us;

giving us a feeling that this should have been going on for a long time. Evan's arms were tightly wrapped around my shoulders. Basking in each other's ambiance, creating each other's warmth. He looked down at me, his eyes dulled by the darkness of the room. He flashed me his crooked smile, the one that reminded me of the first day we met.

Caressing my supple cheek, he lifted my chin; our noses were almost touching. I could feel the warmth of his breath brushing the top of my lip. I stared back into his piercing blue eyes. Flashbacks attacked my eyes with every blink. After every fight and laugh, every tear I shed, I could not wait another moment. Grabbing his shirt, I closed the gap between our lips with one swift movement.

"I'm sorry," I said quietly. I walked away from him, turning to the window. "Gosh, I just ruined everything," I muttered under my breath.

He grabbed me by the wrist and pulled me into a tight hug. "It's okay," he said. "It's okay."

"I miss Margo," I whispered.

"I know," he said. "What if we visited her later?"

"What would Arden say?" I said softly, growing tense.

"Who cares what Arden will say?"

~~~

Later that day we met in front of Margo's door. I took in a deep breath, gripping onto Evan's palm. His fingers intertwined with mine. He looked over at me with this smile. It was a small smile, but the only genuine one I had seen from him in the time I have known him. It warmed my heart to see that it had reached his eyes, because I had honestly never seen any sort of emotion touch those beautiful blue orbs. He always seemed so distant, using his playfulness to cover it up - but to see this smile...It was something that made me wish that I could relive this moment.

"You ready?" he asked, still grinning.

"As ready as I will ever be." I slowly knocked on the door and twisted the knob. I glanced through the door. The walls were white (which was no surprise because literally everything in the hospital was), along with the ceiling, door, and the bed. Gosh, this room needs some color, I thought to myself. A bench was built into the wall underneath the window where Margo sat with a small book gripped in her hands. Margo's eyes fell on me.

"Hello," she said in a small voice, quickly refocusing herself back to her journal.

"Hey," Evan said. "We wanted to talk."

Margo eyed us suspiciously, lifting herself off the bench and walking towards us. "You see, I'm trying this new thing where I get rid of everything that's toxic in my life," she began. She lifted her arm, showing us her yellow band. "I did this - without you or Arden dragging me down. For these past few weeks, I have actually been...happy. I'm not letting anyone take that away from me."

I stared at her, emotionless. "Did our friendship mean nothing to you, then?" I asked flatly. "We came here to apologize and you're not making this any easier for me to do."

I looked at her, stopping any emotion from showing. In all of the weeks that I had known her, I never quite understood her. She has always been the quiet type, but when she spoke, her words really meant something. Every day she wore the same plaid button-up flannel with torn jeans. The worst part is that she could be beautiful. After all, she has the face and body for it. But she cut off her hair and dyed it blue. Not to mention that she never wears any makeup. It almost seems as if she is trying to reject society's version of "perfection."

Before I could say anything else, a girl with bright red hair walked inside the room with a beaming grin. "Margo, you'll never believe what Brent just did," she began. Her eyes fell on Evan and I. "Who are your friends?"

"They were just leaving," Margo said.

"Not so fast," the girl said. "Any friend of Margo is automatically a friend of mine."

"I'm Sawyer," I said softly. "And this is Evan."

"I'm Clifford—the great, almighty, awesome, beautiful…"

Margo cut her off. "What do you want, Clifford?"

"Well, you see, our friends are having another party and I wanted to see if you wanted to come."

Margo laughed heartily. "You didn't even need to ask, Cliff. Of course I'll be there!"

Clifford looked at us shortly, and then beck at Margo. "Your friends can come, too."

"I'd rather not—," Margo began, but Evan cut her off.

"We're in," he said quickly.

Margo flashed him the "I'm going to slap you" look and then grunted. "Fine," she said.

Later that night we drive to the party. After a one hour drive consisting of

Clifford talking nonstop about how the so-called "Brent" is such an idiot, and Margo giving Evan death stares, we finally arrive at the house. Silence fills the air shortly. I take in my surroundings, looking at the small house up ahead. A warm light shines out of the windows. I can hear the faint music playing inside.

Walking into parties has always given me sort of an adrenaline rush. When at a party you see all types of people— people from all different backgrounds. It truly feels like anything and everything is possible.

As we weave through the numerous people in the crowd, Clifford whispers something into Margo's ear and then turns to us.

She mouths, "Follow me" and then proceeds to make her way up a set of stairs. The stairs are practically so narrow that I have to walk up them turned to my side. Clifford waves at several people that she can see just at the top of the staircase.

Once we get to the top of the staircase, I see a series of several rooms unfold. Several couches fill the room, along with what feels like a million people. Clifford leans back to whisper something to me, but it's barely audible over the murmur of the voices. The next thing I know, her, along with Margo and Evan, are gone. I am all alone.

I have never quite been good at being in crowds—especially when I am alone. Many people found that fact rather weird judging by the fact that I am a giant, so it is not as if I would be trampled or anything.

I head over to Taylor Zhou, a girl that was a blue band in Memorial Hospital. I have never really talked to her much, but at this point I just want to find a familiar face in the crowd so I will not seem like too much of a loner.

"Sawyer, Sawyer, Sawyer," she began. "Where have you been all my life?" She staggers over to me with a droopy smile painted across her face. Her words are slurred.

"You're drunk," I say, folding my arms.

"Sober enough," she says, laughing. "You just missed all the fun. There was a keg stand."

"Well, that explains why everyone is up here," I reply. "Besides, I don't drink."

Taylor flashes me a lazy grin. "Then you haven't lived a day yet."

I roll my eyes. "Sure thing, Taylor. Just keep telling yourself that."

I spot Evan standing in a corner surrounded by several people. I walk towards him with a smile.

"Sawyer!" he calls out, motioning me over to him.

As I finally manage to get to him, he wraps his arm around me tightly. "Where have you been?" he whispers.

"Oh, nothing much," I retort. "I just got abandoned by you and got stuck with a girl that was too drunk to function."

"Get a room!"

I turn around only to see Clifford blowing kissing faces at us. "Stop being perverts."

My face turns bright red and I pull away from Evan. I mouth the word sorry and then join the circle that everyone is sitting in.

"Where did you guys go?" I ask, slightly annoyed about the fact that less than thirty seconds into the party, I was already ditched by my so-called friends and stuck with an utter drunk.

"Keg stand," a guy says. His hair, dark and lustrous, has a sheen like fine hardwood. But that comparison is not entirely fair, I suppose. Hardwood does not swish gently like his hair does. "My name is Brent, by the way."

Margo notices the hint of annoyance in the tone of my voice. "Relax, Saw," she begins. "It's not like we were gone for that long."

Clifford laughs. "Guys, want to play a game?"

Everyone in the circle nods, but Evan flashes me an uneasy look.

"What game?" a girl with blonde hair asks.

"Truth or Dare," Clifford answers. "What is a party without Truth or Dare?"

Brent quickly speaks up. "I'll go first," he offers. "Truth or dare, Melissa?"

The blonde girl grins mischievously. "Dare."

Brent pauses for a minute and then speaks again. "I dare you to let me draw on your face with a sharpie." Long story short, Brent wrote Dumb Blonde right on Melissa's forehead and she never picked a dare again.

Eventually it is Clifford's turn and she turns to Margo. "Truth or Dare?" she asks.

"Truth."

"Predictable," Clifford mumbles. Margo sticks her tongue at her. "Okay, what are you afraid of?"

"Myself," she says softly.

"What was that?" Clifford asks.

"It's nothing," she says.

After several other people go, it's Brent's turn again. "Sawyer, Truth or Dare?"

"Dare," I say.

"I dare you to jump into the pool with your clothes on."

I have not even realized that there was a back yard, let alone a pool in the house. "Deal," I say.

He leads me outside onto the balcony, followed by everyone else. "There," he says, pointing at the pool. The water is a bright shade of blue. Almost aquamarine. I am surprised to see that no one is outside. Then again, the majority of the guests are still surrounding the keg upstairs.

I walk towards the edge of the pool, looking at the water. I take in a deep breath and clench my fists.

"Anytime now, Red Band," Clifford taunts.

I take in a big gulp of air and jump. The water thoroughly chills me to the bone.

The icy wind makes my face turn cherry red. The next thing I know, everyone else has jumped into the pool, surrounding me.

Clifford cheers and once she does, everyone else follows suit. "Welcome to our group, Red Band," I hear her say. Everyone slowly moves towards us with beaming grins on their faces. We all splash each other. I do not think I have ever laughed more.

And in that moment I swear, life might just be worth living.

Mari Taylor

PART TWO: PERHAPS

"The fact that man knows right from wrong proves his intellectual superiority to the other creatures; but the fact that he can do wrong proves his moral inferiority to any creatures that cannot."

—*Mark Twain*

*"I want to say somewhere: I've tried to be forgiving.
And yet. There were times in my life, whole years,
when anger got the better of me. Ugliness turned
me inside out. There was a certain satisfaction in
bitterness. I courted it. It was standing outside, and
I invited it in."*

—*Nicole Kruass*

CHAPTER 7: EVAN

They say that a single choice...a single moment can change your life forever. They also say that once you have a near-death experience, you begin to see life through a completely new perspective. I have always liked to imagine that once my time came, I would think about the best memories I have shared with my loved ones. Like jumping in the pool last night—which opened up new opportunities for new (and better) friends, or the time Sawyer and I first laid eyes on each other.

Of course, being the cynical person I am, I would most likely think of all of the pain I have caused my loved ones. I'd recall the time I lost every single one of my best friends because they "couldn't watch me kill myself slowly;" the time my mom and dad told me that they couldn't trust my anymore; the time I was diagnosed with anorexia nervosa; the time my father told me that no son of his would be "anorexic;" the time I was kicked off the football team due to my declining weight.

I remembered the first time I ever encountered a near-death experience. It was my sophomore year of high school, and I fainted on the football field during practice due to a potential lung failure. They told me that at the rate I was going, I most likely would not make it to senior year. I remember waking up in the hospital angry—mad at the word for letting me live. When I was little my older sister, Alana, would tell me "everything happens for a reason." And as for the reason I am still alive despite the fact that I have come dangerously near to the great visit from the Grim Reaper... I am not quite sure yet what that reason is. But, hey—that's just life, isn't it? Life is a book, and there are 1000 pages that I have not yet read.

I opened my eyes, still lying in my bed, and stayed like that for a few minutes. I tried to make sense of what happened last night, but it all seemed a mess in my mind. The sun was dappled through the window, streaming through.

"Hey," a familiar voice broke my thoughts. I sat up rapidly, my heart racing. It was Arden. "You ignored all of my texts and calls yesterday. Where were you?"

I yawned, sliding the covers off me and paused for a moment. "Um, I was with Sawyer and a couple of friends."

"A couple of friends?" she repeated with a hint of sarcasm in her voice. "Other than Sawyer, I am your only friend."

I looked at her blankly, restraining all emotion. "Get out," I said as calmly as I could manage.

Constantly, Arden would make comments such as that. Up until now, I had overlooked them, but today was different. I tried thinking of all the positive memories we shared together, her benevolent smile, and the way she laughed when I told her my cheesy jokes. However, it still did not work. I looked into her eyes, thinking of all the memories that we once shared.

Arden spoke after several moments of silence. "I'm sorry," she sighed and continued, "So I can try and make this better for the both of us."

Only silence followed and I still refused to speak. With each passing minute, each second taunted and nagged at her. Her face was becoming crimson, and her eyes seemed to spark with fury. Her once passive features were consumed by rage and anger, resentment and wrath. Her speech became sarcastic, acrimonious even.

"So that's it?" she said harshly. "You're not even going to speak to me?"

I still did not say anything and just looked outside the window of my bedroom, trying to distract myself from saying or doing anything that I would regret. Her gaze met mine, forming an intense stare.

"Arden, no!" I spewed out, the words tasting like bile. "I'm tired of your games. Don't you see that it's killing us?" She stared at me blankly, empty of all emotion.

"Are you heartless," I continued, nearly screaming. "Sawyer…Margo… myself — we all came here to recover, but you are just dragging us further down."

Bitterly, she said, "I'm saying I'm sorry. We can fix this." At that point, she was on the verge of tears. "Evan, you are one of my closest friends, and I need you in my life. There, I said it. Are you happy now?"

I said nothing in response.

"You can erase me from your life—you can act like I don't exist, but that doesn't change the memories you gave me. That doesn't change the fact that I care about you more than I care about myself." Her voice trailed off. "So there you have it. Ignore me, talk to me, whatever."

She paused. "You're just like Tyler, did you know that?"

"Who?" I asked.

"My brother," she said, staring at the ground. A single drop of grief welled up from the corner of her eye and suddenly, the dam broke. "Everyone leaves me— no matter who or how close we were. I always end up being left by someone as soon as I let my guard down and get close to them."

I found myself at a loss of words. "I'm sorry," I whispered.

"No," she said, voice breaking. "There's going to be a day when you lose someone who was once your whole world. And when that happens, don't come to me crying."

And just like that, she was gone, leaving me standing in my room still processing what just occurred.

~~~

"It's gotten to a point where I don't know who I am anymore," I said. "I constantly feel like I'm on the verge of breaking down—I feel as if I'm going crazy. I cannot sleep. I can't concentrate, let alone think straight."

Every day at noon, I would have a session with Mrs. Sue, my therapist. She nodded and swiftly scribbled something down in her notebook. I uneasily looked around her spacious office, trying to distract myself from any thought of what happened earlier.

"How have you been doing, Evan?" she asked.

~~I am coming apart at the seams and it scares me~~.

"I'm fine," I lie, staring at the ground.

"I know recovery seems nearly impossible," she began. "But I promise you that everything will be okay."

~~Yeah, because it is not happening to you~~.

"Thanks," I said softly.

"So, have you been making friends while staying here?"

As soon as she asked me that, thoughts of Arden suddenly came to mind.

My brother, she said, staring at the ground. A single drop of grief welled up from the corner of her eye and suddenly, the dam broke.

Everyone leaves me—no matter who or how close we were. I always end up being left by someone as soon as I let my guard down and get close to them.

"You could say something like that," I said softly.

"You religious?" Mrs. Sue asked after a few moments of silence.

"Is that really appropriate for—," I began, but she cut me off.

"Are you religious?" she asked again, but this time firmer.

"Yeah," I said, still taken off-guard by her question.

"Well," she began. "A wise person— who was once a minister—once said 'we all have our demons, but they don't make us who we are as a person; how we handle them does.'"

"What does that have to do with anything?" I almost snorted.

Ignoring my question, Mrs. Sue said, "Have you ever tried focusing on recovery by channeling your energy on something you enjoy doing?"

I shook my head. "No, not really."

"You're friends with Margo Sanchez, right?"

You see, I'm trying this new thing where I get rid of everything that's toxic in my life," she began. She lifted her arm, showing us her yellow band. "I did this-- without you or Arden dragging me down. For these past few weeks, I have actually been... happy. I'm not letting anyone take that away from me.

"You could say something like that," I said.

Mrs. Sue nodded, "Well, ever since I recommended that she start focusing on writing, she's moved up from red band to nearly green band. Maybe you could try focusing on a skill you have."

~~Maybe I do not want to recover.~~ "That seems great," I said.

After a few moments of silence, she finally asked, "Do you have any hobbies?"

"I like to party - and by party, I mean take naps." I let out a small laugh and continued. "I listen to music quite a lot, and I dabble in filmmaking here and there."

"Well, maybe you could create a YouTube channel or—"

I let out a dry laugh. "Yes, because *everyone* wants to hear probably the only guy ever diagnosed with anorexia nervosa talk to himself through a camera."

"There's Brent," Mrs. Sue said, trying to keep herself from laughing.

"Except Brent is a wild animal. There's a difference between he and I."

She chuckled. "Okay, Evan," she said. "That will be all for today."

"Life is like riding a bicycle. To keep your balance, you must keep moving."

—Albert Einstein

CHAPTER 8: ARDEN

Breathe in. Breathe out. Breathe in. Breathe out. Breathe in. Breathe out. Breathe in. Breathe out. Breathe in. Breathe out. Breathe in. Breathe out. Breathe in. Breathe out. Breathe in. Breathe out. Breathe in. Breathe out. Breathe in. Breathe out. Breathe in. Breathe out. Breathe in. Breathe out. Breathe in. Breathe out. Breathe in. Breathe out. Breathe in. Breathe out. Breathe in. Breathe out. Breathe in. Breathe out.

Breathe in. Breathe out. Breathe in. Breathe out.

Sometimes I feel as if I have to remind myself of this every day…Sometimes I feel as if I have to remind myself to keep **moving**; to keep **talking**; to keep **living.** Sometimes I think to myself, *is continuing this fight for recovery even worth it?*

Today was the first time in months that I've actually been able to visit my family at their home—it was the first time in months I've been able to face Tyler since our last argument.

Breathe in. Breathe out.

I remember the last time I ever spoke to my brother. It was ages ago, yet I remember it like it was just yesterday:

"I'm tired of your bullshit, Arden," Tyler *spat out. His once hazel eyes that were filled with nothing but kindness were now hardened and emotionless.*

"Tyler-," I began, but he cut me off.

"No,' he said firmly. "Do you not understand what you are doing to mum and dad? They cannot handle watching you die slowly. You're breaking them inside."

Hot and salty tears ran down my face. "I'm sorry," I managed to get out.

"I don't have a little sister anymore," he said. "She left me a long time ago. Now I just have an eating disorder living down the hall."

I tried to say something...anything, but only uncontrollable sobs came out. "At the rate you're going now, you will die soon. I don't want to stick around and watch that happen." He turned away from me, facing his bedroom door.

"Tyler, please," I begged. My voice was practically a whisper, barely audible over my faint cries. "I'M SORRY!" I yelled with all of the strength that I had left into the darkness of the night.

"Screw you, Arden." his voice was strong, but it trembled. His lips gave in, he let out a small cry of guilt, and sadness overwhelmed him. "All you've ever done is make life for mum and dad a living hell."

Breathe in. Breathe out.

How could I ever forget Tyler's last words?

"All you've ever done is make life for mum and dad a living hell."

I live with them every single day. I deal with them as I **move.** I deal with them as I **talk.** I deal with them as I **think**. I deal with them as I **live.** I deal with them as I **breathe in.** I deal with them as I **breathe out.**

I guess that is just something that I will always have to live with. His words will always be bound to me—irreversible from my memory.

~~~

Later that day I finally arrived at my house. I took a breath in and knocked on the door, which might have been one of the most nerve-wracking things I have ever done.

"Arden," my mom said. Tears streamed down her eyes as she smiled. She wrapped her arms around me tightly. It was painless. Her arms gripped me, leaving me breathless as she held onto me. I relived our past memories in the comfort of her arms. I remembered when she would take Tyler, dad, and I out bobbing for apples every fall; I remembered how she would sing songs to me every time things got hard. It seems as if I had lost all memory of the pain I caused everyone, and only thought of the few cheerful times we shared. With one last choking squeeze, I let go of the light that made my darkness fade and remained floating on the emotional high of our bond.

"Dinner is set at the table," she began. "Why don't you go get settled? The food should be ready any minute now."

Dinner. Food. Fat. Calories.

"I'm not very hun—"I began, but then I stared into my mom's light grey eyes. She gave me a look that read: *please, just once.*

I quickly nodded and then made my way into the kitchen. Tyler sat the table, staring down at the floor.

"Hey," I said, trying to break the silence.

No answer.

"Tyler, you're going to talk to me sometime."

No answer.

Breathe in. Breathe out. Breathe in. Breathe out. Breathe in. Breathe out. Breathe in. Breathe out. Breathe in. Breathe out. Breathe in. Breathe out. Breathe in. Breathe out. **Breathe in. Breathe out**.

"Tyler, please," I said softly.

He looked up at me coldly. "You want me to say something?" he said. "What else is there to say?"

I shrugged. "I just figured that you would have forgiven me by now…"

"Forgiveness?" he mimicked. "How can I forgive someone that ruined my life?"

"I'm sorry," I said. "But don't you miss your sister by now? It's been months."

"I lost my sister a long time ago," he said, walking out of the kitchen.

Breathe in. Breathe out. Breathe in. Breathe out. Breathe in. Breathe out. Breathe in. Breathe out. Breathe in. Breathe out. Breathe in. Breathe out. Breathe in. Breathe out. Breathe in. Breathe out. Breathe in. Breathe out. Breathe in. Breathe out. Breathe in. Breathe out. Breathe in. Breathe out. **Breathe in. Breathe out.**

Dinner mostly consisted of small talk - Mom and Dad pretending everything was fine in their marriage, Tyler ignoring me, and Mom asking me to eat my food.

I honestly wish that I could eat like a normal person does. I wish that I could eat an entire apple without feeling the slightest form of guilt. Maybe then, Mom and Dad's marriage would be fixed, and Tyler would actually speak to me again.

Out of all of the crappy life lessons, I have learned in my 17 years, I have learned that things just do not always turn out how you want them to. No matter how much you wish on a star that does not mean that your hopes and dreams suddenly become reality. For now, all I can do is breathe in and breathe out.

Breathe in. Breathe out. Breathe in. Breathe out. Breathe in. Breathe out. Breathe in. Breathe out. Breathe in. Breathe out. Breathe in. Breathe out. Breathe in. Breathe out. Breathe in. Breathe out. Breathe in. Breathe out. Breathe in. Breathe out. Breathe in. Breathe out. Breathe in. Breathe out. Breathe in. Breathe out. Breathe in. Breathe out. Breathe in. Breathe out. Breathe in. Breathe out.

Breathe in. Breathe out. Breathe in.
Breathe out. **Breathe in. Breathe out.**

"The truth is, unless you let go, unless you forgive yourself, unless you forgive the situation, unless you realize that the situation is over, you cannot move forward."

—*Steve Maraboli*

CHAPTER 9: MARGO

Dear journal, it has been a while since I have last written. I guess one could say that I have been busy with…I don't know: books, boring parties, and dealing with obnoxious drunks—whatever teens do these days.

Mrs. Sue says that at the rate I am going, I just might be able to leave in the next two months. Just the thought of going home amazes me. I have not talked to my parents in ages—let alone visited them. To tell you the truth, I honestly do not want to go home.

Dealing with my parents just is not something I am sure I am quite ready to do yet. Since the eating has gone to hell, though, I know I will probably have to stay a bit longer. Anyways, that is probably all the time I will have to write today.

Take care, Margo.

~~~

Have I ever mentioned how itchy the standard medical gowns we're required to wear are? I quickly slipped one on and began to head down for my daily checkup. I groaned, still exhausted from writing nearly all night.

As I walked down the cold hallway, I noticed a few people waiting miserably near a few nurses. I joined them, leaning against an open space next on the bare white wall. Although each one of us was significantly different, one thing we all shared was our grim facial expression, which reflected absolute dread. No one was fond of the 6 a.m. checkups. Honestly, the nurses themselves seemed to dread them as well.

"Margo," a nurse called as a girl exited her office. It was Arden. Our eyes met shortly, but then I dropped mine to the floor quickly. Her eyes were red and puffy. She looked as if she wanted to say something, but then she paused, and walked away.

"You know the drill by now, Blue," the nurse said. I stepped on the scale, taking in a deep breath. The nurse nodded and gave me permission to step off.

"So what is it today?" I asked.

"111," she said with a slight grin. "Nice work, Blue." She handed me a bright green band. "Pretty soon you might just be able to get out of this place."

I laughed. "Thanks," I said, heading out of her office.

Once I arrived at my room, I grabbed a few clothes and headed to the bathrooms down the hall. I ran my hand along the showerhead and made the water scalding hot. The response was immediate; the metallic head that hung loosely above me spread water onto my body, the sudden shock causing my muscles to tense.

The water slowly warmed me, soothing the ache that clawed at my limbs. A tear trickled down my cheek and mixed with the clean water as I poured gentle soap into my hands.

Home, I thought. *I am finally going home.* My fingers met short blue hair, untangling my curls, ridding it of the knots time had caused. I have honestly never thought of home. Being here so long, I never knew that recovery was even possible. I dragged the soap over my body, the action soothing my tough skin. It reminded me of the time I was actually at home. Home has really seemed like a foreign word to me. For such a long time, this place has been home for me.

Clifford...Brent...Sawyer...Evan. When I was with them, it always felt like a home enough to me. More tears escaped my eyes, followed by my fist meeting the wall. Somewhere, above surface, the young girl inside of me dropped to the floor, letting the water caress my skin as I broke down and wept. When I was alone, I felt truly free. I felt as if there was no more use for the barriers I built up, and they all came crumbling down.

I slowly stepped out of the shower, wrapping a towel tightly around me. I took a brief look at the mirror across the room.

~~My collarbone was less noticeable.~~
~~Imperfection. Imperfection.~~
~~Imperfection.~~

I pulled my hair up into a messy bun and briefly applied some makeup.

"Hurry up," I heard someone call. It was my nurse. "You're going to miss breakfast."

"Coming," I called out and quickly slipped on my clothes.

~~~

If you could imagine a place—a place where people of all backgrounds sat together in complete and utter silence, that would be Memorial Hospital's cafeteria.

I hastily walked over to the counter, carefully analyzing the different foods available. I filed my tray with an egg, a small cup of fruit, yogurt, and a glass of milk.

Carefully placing my tray at a table where Sawyer, Evan, Brent, and Clifford sat, I began to start eating the cup of fruit.

60 calories.

I slowly began chewing on a small blueberry.

60 calories.

Then I ate a grape.

60 calories.

One strawberry.

60 calories.

Three pineapples.

60 calories.

Margo, stop. It was the voice of Ana, also known as anorexia. Ever since I began writing, I had not really heard much from her.

Taking in a deep breath, I continued eating my food.

Three grapes.

60 calories.

Keep going, Margo, I told myself. Finally, I finished the cup of fruit and then reached for the cup of yogurt.

90 calories.

I ate several spoonfuls, and then stopped.

"I'll take your tray for you," Evan said.

I nodded. "Thanks."

~~~

"Want to go on a jog?" Arden asked.

I rested my back against a tree outside, still waiting for Clifford and the others to return from their group session. "Haven't heard you say that in a while," I said, ignoring her question. "Why are you here?"

"I miss you guys," she said. "What happened to us?"

"Life did," I answered. "It's clear that you have different motives than I do when it comes to staying here."

She sighed. "Can we at least talk?"

"A wise man once said, "'It's hard to say goodbye to the streets. It is all how you do it. You can pass by and say, 'What's happening?' and keep it moving, but it's a certain element that'll never be able to roll with you once you get to this level because that's the separation of it all."

"Who said that?"

"Snoop Dogg."

She laughed. It has been a while since I have last seen her smile like that. It seemed like for a moment—a brief one, at that—but she seemed happy. All of the pain in her eyes suddenly seemed to disappear.

"Margo, I want things to go back the way they were," she began. "I want it to be like when it was when it was just you, me, and Evan."

"Do you not realize how it was like when I was with you?"

She shook her head.

"It was hell. You only brought me deeper and deeper into my eating disorder. Every time I would try to get better, you would only drag me deeper into your downward spiral."

She stared at me blankly, emotion draining from her face.

"You know what, I forgive you. I forgive you because I'm tired of staying angry," I said. "I forgive you even after the shit you brought me through."

Still no answer. She merely mumbled, "It's not fair."

I lifted myself off the ground and looked her right in the eyes. "I know life is unfair, and I know things may seem hard. I also know that you are expecting me to say 'it will get better', But I'm not going to tell you that," I began. "To tell you the truth, life is messed up—the choices we make, the people we associate with, it's just one giant mess. Things can be are hard. Things can be pathetic, but that's just life."

She looked at the ground, wiping away a single tear.

I continued. "I know it hurts... I know recovery hurts. I even know that along the way, you just might lose some people that you once were very close to. However, that's life. That is the tragic, yet beautiful thing about it. It may not matter now, but one day you will wake up, say, 'I made it', and realize that there is someone out there. That there is someone out there that loves you. Trust me, you will find yourself again. Just like I did."

"But that's the thing," she said. "Life doesn't always get better for everyone."

Before I could say anything else, she walked away.

~~~

"You know what a bunch a bullshit this is?" Sawyer asked.

"Whoa, watch the language Red Band," Clifford teased.

Instead of going to a party tonight, we all decided to go starwatching in the field out in the back of Memorial Hospital. It was nice (and not to mention drunk-free, which automatically made it 1000 times nicer).

"For your information, I'm actually a yellow band," Sawyer said. She lay on the ground next to Evan, her hands gripping loosely onto his. The faint moonlight reflected against her ebony skin and dark almond eyes.

"Sure thing, Red Band," Brent said.

We all laughed.

"Have you guys ever wondered what it would be like once we got home?" I asked.

"Well, the first thing I would do is throw the biggest party anyone has ever seen," Brent said.

"Wow, such a shocker," Sawyer mocked.

"Cool it, Red Band."

Every night we all hung out, things would start out great. We all would talk about anything and everything. That is until we ran out of things to stay happy about. Clifford would try to keep us in high spirits, but even at times, she herself had struggles staying positive about our situation.

"Arden tried to talk to me today," I said after a few moments of silence. I am not quite sure exactly why I decided to share that. After all, it is not like it mattered or anything.

"I haven't spoken to her in weeks," Evan said. "What did she say?"

"She asked me if we could go on a jog," I said. "After that, she asked if we could talk about things going back to normal."

"What did you say," he asked.

"I said no, but then told her that I forgive her."

"Why is that?" Brent asked.

"I was tired of staying angry at her. Hell, she probably deserved for me to stay mad forever. I guess it's just better letting some things go," I said. "After all, how can I recover if I'm stuck living in the past?"

"I didn't want to wake up. I was having a much better time asleep. And that's really sad. It was almost like a reverse nightmare, like when you wake up from a nightmare you're so relieved. I woke up into a nightmare."

—Ned Vizzinni

CHAPTER 10: SAWYER

MY eyes darted open. As they focused, I noticed it was just my weary bedroom. I was shaking to the bone and whispering to myself, *thank goodness it was only a nightmare*. I sat up and tears poured down my cheeks. I threw myself to the ground as I let all the overwhelming emotions go. All the pain, sorrow and agony in this one simple noise. Quickly, I took in short, quick breaths.

Society Killed the Cat

Worthless, scum, stupid, the voices echoed through my mind. I reached over to my alarm clock. 6:30, it read. It was time for the morning checkup and I was already late.

If there were one thing I hated most about Memorial Hospital, it would have to be the checkups. I quickly slipped on my itchy hospital gown and headed down the hallway.

Once it was my turn to go into the nurse's office, I stepped on the scale hastily.

Worthless, scum, stupid, the voices echoed through my mind.

"106," the nurse said. "That's two pounds less than last time." She gave me a concerned look momentarily, and then scribbled something down on her notebook.

"I guess I've just been tired lately," I said, shrugging.

The nurse sighed. "You should hurry up," she began. "You'll be late for breakfast."

Don't, something inside of me said, *Skip breakfast and go straight to the showers.* I am not quite sure why I listened. I sighed and walked inside the bathrooms. I stepped into the shower and allowed the cool water to relax my tense muscles.

Worthless, scum, stupid, the voices echoed through my mind.

A single tear trickled down my cheek as I poured some soap into my hand. ~~Maybe the voices are right. I am worthless...fat...ugly...weak.~~

I ran my hands through my hair, attempting to keep myself from tears.

Fat, ugly, worthless, scum, disgusting, fake, idiot.

After my shower, I wrapped a towel around me and turned to the sink.

"Hey."

I spun around, gasping. It was Arden. "What the hell, Arden! You scared the crap out of me," I sputtered.

She gave me a weak smile. "Sorry," she said. "I didn't see you at breakfast this morning."

"I guess I was just tired," I said, shrugging.

~~I was tired of feeling alone. I was tired of recovery. I was tired of crying myself to sleep. I was crying. I was tired of hurting people. I was tired of losing people. I was tired of losing my mind. I was tired of losing myself. I was tired of not being able to get through recovery. I was tired of being different. Nevertheless, most of all, I was tired of being tired.~~

A few moments of silence passed. I looked at her awkwardly, raising my eyebrows a bit. "Want to go on a jog?" I asked.

~~~

I weaved through the trees, which bordered the perimeter of the field out back. It was not my first time being admitted into the hospital. Arden trailed near behind me. After staying here for so long, I already knew the ins and outs of the field and what surrounded its shore.

Cresting a hill towards the far back of the field, I broke free of a dense patch of needle leaves and rolled freely down the embankment, a natural landslide that served my purposes more effectively now that it was covered in snow. I sped ahead of Arden, escaping the observant gaze of her people.

Running had always exhilarated me; allowed me a freedom seldom experienced in my station. Behind the cloak of darkness, I could run like the tall-horned stag, waving his white tail in a gesture of peace instead of alarm.

As the canopy overhead thickened, my steps grew muffled by the pine needles that blanketed the grassy floor; the ground was no longer cold beneath my soles. I paused to take a breath.

Fat, ugly, worthless, idiot.

I had honestly forgotten how much I loved to run. The way the fresh air coursed through my lungs; the way my legs stung after running for a long period of time; the way I felt free of all problems—it all gave me sort of an adrenaline rush.

After running around the perimeter of the field several times, Arden and I finally came back inside for dinner. I told Arden goodbye and headed back to my room. Evan stood at my door, arms crossed.

"Hey," I said, giving him a quick hug.

Fat, ugly, worthless, idiot.

"Where were you?" he asked. "I've been looking for you all day."

Do not tell him.

"Partying, going to clubs," I said. "I don't know—whatever teens do these days."

"I didn't see you at breakfast today," he said. "Or at lunch."

I gave him a reassuring smile. "I'm fine, Evan," I said. "I've just been out."

"Has anyone ever told you that you are a really bad liar?"

I rolled my eyes and walked inside my room, trying to give him a sign that I did not want to talk anymore. Unfortunately, he did not catch my (*oh, so subtle*) sign and followed me.

"You were with Arden again, weren't you?"

I turned my back on him, facing the small window towards the back of my room.

I glanced out the rain-speckled window, drinking in the sight of the small droplets hitting the pavement. I know I spend too much time staring out my window, wondering what lies ahead. To me, it is an escape from all of the problems that I have to live with every day of my life. I do not know why I do this to myself. I do not know why I spend so much time imagining that life gets better, when in reality, it does not. It must be some sort of a sick game, which is for my own amusement.

"Answer me, Sawyer."

I continued to stare out the window, ignoring Evan's calls in favor of gazing at the colorless sky. "I really don't see why you should care where I was."

"Maybe because I'm worried?" He said. His voice rose, shaking with a hint of anger. He paused. "Whatever I say won't make a difference, anyways."

I turned around, looking him straight in the eyes. "Do you think I have a problem?"

He nodded. "It's not like you'll listen, anyways, so what's the point of explaining?"

I felt frustrated but more than that, I could not believe the words he just said. I could not believe someone that I once told everything... someone who was family to me, someone I had trusted, would say that to me. My tears just ran, and I tried forcing them back, but they came down anyway, flooding over the feelings I used to have for him.

"I hate you," I mumbled.

His eyes widened. My stomach dropped. I instantly felt regret. The thing about regret is that it is not about what you do. It is about what you did not do. I **did not** tell Evan *sorry*. I **did not** tell Evan what was wrong. I **did not** tell Evan about my weight dropping.

A few moments of silence passed. "I'm sorry," I said, tears rolling down my cheek. "I didn't mean—"

He cut me off. "Of course you didn't mean to say it," he began. "You never think of anyone but yourself nowadays—don't you?" He stared at the floor, trying to stay calm. "I don't think that this is going to work out."

Fat, ugly, worthless, idiot.

"What do you mean?" I asked.

"Us. I think that we should take a break," he continued. "Sometimes you just need a break—in a beautiful place. Alone. It gives us time to focus on recovery."

He does not want you anymore because you are fat... stupid... ugly...worthless.

"Go," I said in a soft whisper.

At first, he attempted to apologize, but eventually he left—just as everyone does.

I stood there for a moment, feeling numb. I headed to the showers to get ready for bed. When I walked in, I stopped in front of the mirror. Most days I often found it hard to look at my own reflection. At times, I would stare at myself, wondering if people would miss me if I were gone. I often end up crying myself to sleep every night. I am so sad, yet even I do not even know why.

However, I got out of bed today. That's a start.

Before I walked into the shower, Clifford walked in with a beaming smile across her face.

"Hey, Red Band," she said. "I haven't seen you all day."

"I've been out," I said, giving her a weak smile.

"Well, there's a party at Taylor's tonight—you remember her right?"

I nodded. "I guess I'll be there," I said. ~~Only if it gets the thought of Evan out of my head.~~

"Cool," she said. "I'll give you a ride. Margo is coming with us, too."

~~~

The party was just getting started when we arrived. I headed out to the backyard to get some fresh air.

Whenever I go outside on the dead, lonely nights, I feel very vulnerable to my surroundings. However, this night was different. I felt a sense of being dead inside, numb of all feelings. The sky was dark. Rain still drizzled from the night sky, hitting me lightly.

I looked up into the sky where it seemed as if there was no space or time, and where everything looked so serene and calm. Everything up there just floated like a balloon, free to be itself. No pressure. No need to be bound by anyone else's expectations.

"Got a cigarette?" I heard someone ask. I turned around, only to see Arden leaning against a wall.

I shook my head. "What are you doing here?"

"I was invited by a friend," she said. "And you?"

"Clifford," I sighed.

A moment of silence passed, which seemed like forever.

"Evan broke up with me," I said. I am not quite sure why I said it, but I felt as if I needed to get it off my chest.

She shook her head, sighing. "What happened?"

In that moment I thought of what happened before:

"I hate you," I mumbled.

*His eyes widened. My stomach dropped. I instantly felt regret. The thing about regret is that it is not about what you do. It is about what you did not do. I **did not** tell Evan sorry. I **did not** tell Evan what was wrong. I **did not** tell Evan about my weight dropping.*

A few moments of silence passed. "I'm sorry," I said, tears rolling down my cheek. "I didn't mean—"

He cut me off. "Of course you didn't mean to say it," he began. "You never think of how your words could affect others." He stared at the floor, trying to stay calm. "I don't think that this is going to work out."

Fat, ugly, worthless, idiot.

"What do you mean?" I asked.

"I think that we need to take a break," he continued. "Sometimes you just need a break—in a beautiful place. Alone. It gives us time to focus on recovery."

He does not want you anymore because you are fat...stupid ugly... worthless.

"Go," I said in a soft whisper. At first, he attempted to apologize, but eventually he left—just as everyone does.

~~~

"Sawyer?" Arden asked again.

"He just ended it," I said, my voice breaking.

"You still love him, don't you?" she asked.

"I do," I said. "And maybe he still loves me, but I can't escape the fact that I'll never be good enough for him. I should have expected it to happen at some point. So, I'm not going to blame him for breaking it off. I am not angry either. Hell, I should be furious, but I'm not. I just feel numb—really numb."

She looked at me, smiling a bit. "Life screws us all over. Doesn't it?" she said, laughing. "But that's that beauty of it. One day you will wake up next to the one you love and realize that it is going to be all right. You'll realize that tomorrow is worth living, and once you get there, whatever happened today won't matter a bit."

"Thanks for that," I said. "I'm going to get a drink. I'll be back."

She nodded as I turned to open the door next to her. The moment I opened the door, I froze. Evan.

He looked at me for a moment and began to walk towards me.

"Of course you didn't mean to say it," he began. *"You never think of anyone but yourself—don't you?" He stared at the floor, trying to stay calm. "I don't think that this is going to work out."*

Fat, ugly, worthless, idiot.

"What do you mean?" I asked.

"Us. I think that we should take a break," he continued. *"Sometimes you just need a break—in a beautiful place.*

Alone. It gives us time to focus on recovery."

My heart pounded harder than I could ever remember. My eyesight was beginning to blur, tears forming as he stared at me. Time seemed to crawl by slower as he got closer and closer to me. Wiping away a few tears that ran down my cheeks, I flew through the door, running, trying to escape. Arden and Evan soon trailed behind me. I looked up ahead and ran towards the woods behind Taylor's house.

Cold, damp air brushed against my hair, exposing it to all things around me. I heard tapping in a nearby bush, and saw what seemed like a shadow, I wasn't sure. I heard voices behind me, calling my name. I heard a rattle above me; looking up, I almost fell from the stunning sight. The moon, like a milky face in the sky, was serving as a gigantic flashlight to guide my way. Rotten leaves and twigs crushed under my two feet, as I began running across the forest looking for a place to get out.

"Of course you didn't mean to say it," he began. *"You never think of anyone but yourself—don't you?" He stared at the floor, trying to stay calm. "I don't think that this is going to work out."*

Fat, ugly, worthless, idiot.

"What do you mean?" I asked.

"Us. I think that we should take a break," he continued. "Sometimes you just need a break—in a beautiful place. Alone. It gives us time to focus on recovery."

"Keep running," I muttered under my breath. "Just keep running."

"You see, I'm trying this new thing where I get rid of everything that's toxic in my life," Margo began. She lifted her

arm, showing us her yellow band. "I did this--without you or Arden dragging me down. For these past few weeks, I have actually been... happy. I'm not letting anyone take that away from me."

Keep running. Keep moving. Keep running. Keep running. Keep moving. Keep running. Keep running. Keep moving. Keep running. Keep running. Keep moving. Keep running. Keep running. Keep moving. Keep running. Keep running. Keep moving. Keep running.

"Maybe because I'm worried?" Evan said. His voices rose, shaking with a hint of anger. He paused. "Whatever I say won't make a difference, anyways."

Keep running. Keep moving. **Keep running.**

Mari Taylor

"Some people believe holding on and hanging in there are signs of great strength. However, there are times when it takes much more strength to know when to let go and then do it."

—*Ann Landers*

CHAPTER 11: ARDEN

Arden, Sawyer!" I heard the voices of Evan, Margo, Clifford and Brent coming towards us deep in the woods. As I ran towards the faint silhouette of Sawyer, mud splashed on my jeans, ruining them.

"Sawyer!" I yelled. I knew she could not hear me over the sound of the heavy rain. I took in my surroundings, using the faint moonlight as my only source of light. "Sawyer!" I yelled once more.

That time she finally came to a halt.

"Arden," I heard again in the distance. It was Evan. As I began getting closer to her, I heard the sound of cars racing down the nearby highway. When I finally reached Sawyer, I found her hunched over the street's curb, clothes drenched.

"What are you doing here?" she asked flatly. I did not answer but stared at her frail body.

"S-Sawyer, please come back inside," I said. She turned to me, staring at me blankly.

"I said, what the heck are you doing out here?" she said, this time firmly. She shivered, pulling her damp, coarse hair out of her eyes.

"I just want to talk," I said, pulling myself down onto the ground next to her. Her expression softened.

"I have absolutely nothing to say. You're wasting your time." She gazed at the cars on the highway with a slight smirk on her face.

"Arden! Sawyer!" the voices were closer now.

"Sawyer, are you okay?" I asked.

She sighed, "I'm fine. Arden."

"Sawyer-," my voice trailed off.

"You know, all my life I've wondered what it would be like to fly... To soar away from your problems as if they were nonexistent," she began. She stood up, never taking her eyes off the cars in the distance.

"Once Evan broke up with me, I realized something -" Her voice trailed off as she took a step towards the highway. I followed her, suddenly feeling tenser.

"What did you realize?" I asked. She turned to me, eyes watering.

"Angels fly, too." In that split second, she threw herself into the road. She turned to me—and I could have sworn she smiled—just as two cars converged on her, crushing her between them.

~~~

Sawyer was pronounced dead less than eight hours later. I remember feeling numb—unsure of what to say...what to do...how to feel. Evan took it the hardest out of all of us. He rarely spoke anymore, but just sat in his room, staring at the wall.

The doctors tried telling us that her death was instant—peaceful, even. But what is "instant" and how long does it last? One second? Ten seconds? Nothing is instant. She must have felt some pain.

I spent much time in my room, replaying exactly what happened the day she died. I would think this is my fault. I would think I could have saved her.

Today Margo came in my room. Clifford and Brent followed her.

"Hey," she said.

I turned around, waving at her. "Hey."

"We were going out to eat," she continued. "You should come."

"Not hungry," I said.

"You have to come out of your room sometime," Clifford said, sighing.

"Are you sure about that?" I said. "I've been perfectly fine here for the past few days."

Margo futilely tried convincing me to come, but eventually they just left.

~~~

The very day of Sawyer's funeral, Evan sat on his bed staring out the window. I slowly knocked on his door and walked in his room.

"Everyone is waiting for you," I said.

"I'm not going."

"You're not going?" I repeated, voice rising,

He sighed. "No, I'm not."

"And why is that?"

"Because I don't want to see Sawyer." The image of her lifeless body sent chills down my back.

"Why not?" I asked.

"Because I hate her!" His agonized screeches filled the air as they left the room. "She left me without saying goodbye." Tears rolled down his cheeks.

"You can't just forget her," I said, nearly screaming. "Believe it or not, you were a big part of her life, and you need to go to her funeral."

"But it's so hard," he said, his voice breaking. "Knowing that this is my fault."

I seized him by the wrist, pulling him against me. "Don't say that."

"But it is," he whispered.

"It's my fault," I said. "Not yours."

"Why do you say that?" he asked.

"I could have grabbed her," I began. "But I just stood there and watched her jump."

Tears welled up in my eyes. I remember hugging him for what seemed like ages.

"It's okay," he whispered. "We'll get through this."

~~~

Sawyer's funeral was precisely one week after she died. It was held in a church that her whole family apparently attended.

When I first got there with Margo and the others, we all sat in the first row of the sanctuary. For a while, I just sat and watched people go up to the casket. Most of the people there were patients from Memorial Hospital. Others, people I did not even recognize.

Sawyer's parents were standing near the coffin, hugging people as they passed by. I looked them right in the eyes and thought, this is all my fault.

"Did she say anything before she went?" Evan asked me, his whispering voice breaking.

In that second, I remembered exactly what happened less than seven day ago:

"You know, all my life I have wondered what it would be like to fly... To soar away from your problems as if they were nonexistent," she began. She stood up,

never taking her eyes off the cars in the distance.

"Once Evan broke up with me, I realized something -" Her voice trailed off as she took a step towards to highway. I followed her, suddenly feeling tenser.

"What did you realize?" I asked. She turned to me, eyes watering.

"Angels fly, too."

~~~

I shivered. "She told me that—that she's always wondered what it to be like to fly. She's free now."

After watching people pay their respects to Sawyer, I finally decided to walk up to her casket, along with Evan and Margo. The walk to Sawyer's coffin felt long, each step slower than the other. I could see her as I approached the coffin. Her hair parted, just barely, over her face. I stared over her coffin, my eyes watering.

"You're at peace now, Sawyer," I whispered. "You're at peace."

"Unless you have been very, very lucky, you have undoubtedly experienced events in your life that have made you cry. So unless you have been very, very lucky, you know that a good, long session of weeping can often make you feel better, even if your circumstances have not changed one bit."

—*Lemony Snicket*

CHAPTER 12: MARGO

We would like to hear a few words from Sawyer's friends," the pastor said. Clifford went up first, taking in a deep breath.

"We all know that Sawyer liked to laugh; she could have you holding your sides within minutes of entering the room. She had funny catch phrases, and just lived life. So those of you that knew Sawyer would know she would say, 'What are you guys crying for?' While we are sad, I think we should try to laugh and remember her the way she really was. I am going to share some of my memories of the way Sawyer really was.

So Sawyer was a very bright person, but when it came to technology—it was not too pretty. Whenever Sawyer would leave a voicemail, she would say 'Hey, it's Sawyer...you know, your friend'—because I *totally* know someone else named Sawyer! And the girl would forget to hang up once she was done. So, there would be like a whole five minutes of just the sound of her breathing. She would also forget—bless her heart—nearly everything. I would like to think that God created shoulders for people like Sawyer because that girl would probably leave her head at home."

She began crying softly. "So there you all have it. That's how Sawyer should be remembered."

It was my turn next. Clutching my journal tightly, I slowly walked up to the podium. I looked at her body, wiping away a few tears.

"My name is Margo Sanchez. Sawyer was funny, loving, caring," I began. "But most importantly, Sawyer gave me a friendship I never expected to happen. However, in the short time I knew her; she made me feel as if life had a meaning. She cared about me even when I shunned her." My voice broke.

"She stayed by my side—despite the fact that I told her that I wanted nothing to do with her."

"Write about us," Sawyer said with a beaming smile. "Of course, I would be the main character."

I walked towards her body lying in the coffin, wiping away a few tears that rolled down my cheeks. I tore out a single page out of my journal, placing it on her casket.

"I kept my promise," I whispered. "I kept my promise."

Next Evan went up. "Sawyer was loved," he said. Those three words sent chills down the back of my neck.

He continued. "I don't know if that means a lot to you, but I just want you to know that she was loved. Maybe she did not know that herself. Maybe that is the reason we're all here today. But I want you to know that she was loved."

"Sawyer gave me something that I never knew existed—love. She taught me that if you love someone, sometimes you have to let go. I am letting go. After all, she did want to be free. This is not me saying goodbye, nor me saying that I am going to forget all of the memories she gave me. Letting go is not like seeing a long lost friend after twenty years. But it's accepting the fact in a minute's time, someone you once shared memories with—someone you once called your best friend—could become a perfect stranger. We all loved Sawyer. However, a part of loving someone is accepting that it is time to move on. So let us take these memories we had with her and remember. Remember how she is happy now. Remember that she's free."

Last was Arden. She quickly walked up to the podium, taking in a deep breath.

"One thing I remember about Sawyer was that she was filled with life. There was always this certain spark to her eyes, which eventually left. Sometime I wonder why. I wonder why it was her instead of me. I wonder how someone with such potential in life could just abruptly leave—

gone within a second. Then I realize that Sawyer is not gone. I realize that the presence of her memories is still here. We still carry her presence. Sawyer taught me many things. She gave me a friendship when I thought that no one was there for me. Even when my brother and parents rejected me from their family, Sawyer made me feel at home."

She paused, laying her head on the podium. I could hear her faint sobs through the microphone. She eventually lifted her head and began again.

"Out of all of the things Sawyer taught me, one of the most important things she taught me was something that's the only reason I am here today."

She paused again, staring down at the coffin.

"She taught me that despite the trials—
the tribulations, life just may be worth
living."

Mari Taylor

ଓଃ 159

"Learning to let go should be learned before learning to get. Life should be touched, not strangled. You have to relax, let it happen at times, and at others move forward with it. It's like boats. You keep your motor on so you can steer with the current. And when you hear the sound of the waterfall coming nearer and nearer, tidy up the boat, put on your best tie and hat, and smoke a cigar right up 'til the moment you go over. That's a triumph."

—Ray Bradbury

EPILOGUE: EVAN

*D*ear Sawyer, Hey, I know I have not written to you in so long—just as I promised. Nevertheless, I want you to know that I have been doing a lot of thinking lately and I miss you.

It is so strange to think that someone I knew so well...someone I once spent hours talking to could just leave my life in an instant. It is so strange to think that sometimes I go entire days without thinking of you. Sometimes I find it easier to forget. I find it easier to erase all memory of the pain I caused you. But then it hits me, a memory or a call from one of our old friends, and then a full wave of emotion crashes upon me.

Part of me wishes you never left. Part of me wants to hold you again, to kiss you again, and to spend hours of a day talking about pointless things. When I look back at all of what went wrong in our relationship, I find it so easy to forget.

This is not me saying that I regret anything. This is not me saying that those memories you gave me were meaningless. Every relationship has its problems, but that is just life. That's normal. It means that one day I will somehow learn how to love again. A *small part of me just misses having me love you, and you love me back.*

I guess what I am saying is that I forgive you. I forgive you for leaving without saying goodbye. I forgive you for lying to me. I forgive you for pushing me away, despite me trying to help you. I hope that you have found happiness, which was everything I could not give to you. However, one part of me hopes that we both still remember how it was like before our problems and that a part of you misses me too.

I placed the letter under a bright yellow flower next to Sawyer's tombstone. Taking in a deep breath, I walked away from her grave, leaving behind a love that once made my entire life. And in that moment, I realized that things will get better—not instantaneously.

Somehow…someway…**I will get through this.**

The End

AUTHOR QUESTION & ANSWER

Where did your idea for *Society Killed the Cat* come from?

During the time I came up with the idea for *Society Killed the Cat*, I was watching one of my closest friends go through the process of recovery from not only an eating disorder, but also chronic depression. I took the personalities of those that I know (including myself) to develop each character, which represents a different stage of her recovery.

What made you decide to begin writing? Did something or someone inspire you?

In the fifth grade, I had a teacher that absolutely hated me (which was rare, because how could one simply hate the amazing me?). She told me that my writing was horrible and that I would never become a writer, as I dreamed.

Instead of letting her **words get to me**, I decided to spend the next few years perfecting my writing skills in order to prove her wrong. In the next three years, I went on to publish a book at the age of 12, and wrote this novel the next year. I have always lived by the saying that, "You must take the words intended to bring you down as a motivation to prove those that brought you down, wrong."

Who was your favorite character in *Society Killed the Cat*? Why?

To be completely honest, I had a lot of fun writing the character "Clifford." Most of her personality was based off my own, and (and everyone loves me so…).

What made you choose to write *Society Killed the Cat* from several POV's (point of view)?

Before writing this novel, I intended on writing the whole thing from just Arden's point of view. However, then I had more ideas on how to make the characters that surrounded her more realistic by exploring their own stories. This eventually led me to writing it in basically everyone's POV. After all, everyone has a story.

If there were one thing you could accomplish in life, what would it be?

At one point off my life, I once said that before the age of 15 I would publish a novel (completed.) Since then, I have also had several other dreams, among them, to walk on the moon, and reach one million subscribers on my YouTube channel. At this point, anything and everything is possible for me.

QUOTES THAT INSPIRED
SOCIETY KILLED THE CAT

"Mental pain is less dramatic than physical pain, but it is more common and also more hard to bear. The frequent attempt to conceal mental pain increases the burden: it is easier to say "My tooth is aching" than to say "My heart is broken."

—*C.S Lewis*

"Pain is the feeling. Suffering is the effect the pain inflicts. If one can endure pain, one can live without suffering. If one can withstand pain, one can withstand anything. If one can learn to control pain, one can learn to control oneself."

—James Frey

"You will lose someone you can't live without, and your heart will be badly broken, and the bad news is that you never completely get over the loss of your beloved. But this is also the good news. They live forever in your broken heart that does not seal

back up. And you come through. It's like having a broken leg that never heals perfectly—that still hurts when the weather gets cold, but you learn to dance with the limp."

—Anne Lemont

"The battle you are going through is not fueled by the words or actions of others; it is fueled by the mind that gives it importance."

—Shannon L. Alder

"The object of a New Year is not that we should have a new year. It is that we should have a new soul and a new nose; new feet, a new backbone, new ears, and new eyes. Unless a particular man made New Year resolutions, he would make no resolutions. Unless a man starts afresh about things, he will certainly do nothing effective."

—G.K Chesterton

"I am forever engaged in a silent battle in my head over whether or not to lift the fork to my mouth,

and when I talk myself into doing so, I taste only
shame. I have an eating disorder."

—Jenna Morrow

"Love never dies a natural death. It dies because we
do not know how to replenish its source. It dies of
blindness, errors, and betrayals. It dies of illness
and wounds; it dies of weariness, of witherings, of
tarnishings."

—Anias Nin

"The fact that man knows right from wrong proves
his intellectual superiority to the other creatures;
but the fact that he can do wrong proves his moral
inferiority to any creatures that cannot."

—Mark Twain

"I want to say somewhere: I've tried to be forgiving.
And yet. There were times in my life, whole years,
when anger got the better of me. Ugliness turned
me inside out. There was a certain satisfaction in
bitterness. I courted it. It was standing outside, and
I invited it in."

—*Nicole Kruass*

"Life is like riding a bicycle. To keep your balance, you must keep moving."

—*Albert Einstein*

"The truth is, unless you let go, unless you forgive yourself, unless you forgive the situation, unless you realize that the situation is over, you cannot move forward."

—*Steve Maraboli*

"I didn't want to wake up. I was having a much better time asleep. And that's really sad. It was almost like a reverse nightmare, like when you wake up from a nightmare you're so relieved. I woke up into a nightmare."

—*Ned Vizzinni*

"Some people believe holding on and hanging in there are signs of great strength. However, there are times when it takes much more strength to know when to let go and then do it."

—*Ann Landers*

"Unless you have been very, very lucky, you have undoubtedly experienced events in your life that have made you cry. So unless you have been very, very lucky, you know that a good, long session of weeping can often make you feel better, even if your circumstances have not changed one bit."

—*Lemony Snicket*

"Learning to let go should be learned before learning to get. Life should be touched, not strangled. You've got to relax, let it happen at times, and at others move forward with it. It's like boats. You keep your motor on so you can steer with the current. And when you hear the sound of the waterfall coming nearer and nearer, tidy up the boat, put on your best tie and hat, and smoke a cigar right up 'til the moment you go over. That's a triumph."

—*Ray Bradbur*

SOCIETY KILLED THE CAT PLAYLIST

1. ***Breathe Me* by Sia.** *Breathe Me* gets me in touch with exactly how each character is feeling. It gives me a sense of understanding.

2. ***Afraid* by the Neighbourhood.** This song puts me in the place of the characters. It also helps me understand what some of their fears in their situation would be.

3. ***If You Don't Want to Love Me* by James Morrison.** This song helps me understand exactly how Sawyer feels after Evan leaves her.

4. ***Let Me Go* by Hiam.** This song symbolizes the relationship between the main characters and anorexia itself.

5. ***Warrior* by Demi Lovato.** This song represents the shift of the characters' mindsets when they finally decided to pursue recovery.

SOCIETY KILLED THE CAT DISCUSSION QUESTIONS

Synopsis

"I didn't choose to be anorexic—it snuck up on me as a healthy diet and simply something to change my life for the better. But like any drug, anorexia is deadly, but addictive at the same time."

Six teens—one story. Six teens who couldn't be any more different meet at Memorial Hospital, due to being admitted because of their eating disorders. Will this chance meeting be their result in them finding themselves or their ultimate downfall?

In her most powerful and emotional novel yet, Taylor explores the minds of several teens, and how society has twisted the image of what "perfection" truly is. These teens take a very long and painful path to recovery, holding onto the only thing that they have left—hope.

Topics & Questions

1. What is the symbolism between Arden and Sawyer's relationship?

2. How do you think Margo would be affected if she never decided to pursue writing?

3. Out of all of the characters, whom do you identify with most? Why?

4. Is there any character you feel sympathetic for? Why? Why not?

5. Why do you think the author decided to write *Society Killed the Cat* from the point of view of several

characters? How does that affect the book? How would it be different if the author had chosen to write it in only one person's point of view?

6. What do you think that finally makes Sawyer pursue recovery?

7. What do you think leads to Sawyer's ultimate downfall?

8. Discuss the lines, "We all have our demons, but they don't make us who we are as a person, how we handle them does." What do you think that means?

9. Do you think that if things ended differently between Sawyer and Evan, the book would have had a different conclusion??

10. What do you think finally allows Evan to let Sawyer go?

11. Discuss Tyler's appearances in the novel. What do you think about how he reacted to Arden's eating disorder? Would you react any differently? Why or why not?

12. Why do you think Margo finally decides to forgive Arden? Would you have done the same thing? Why or why not?

13. Discuss the following passage: "so how have you been, Margo?' Mrs. Sue, my counselor, asked me.

~~I am tired, hungry, afraid, depressed, broken, sad, lonely, hurt, upset, and angry at the world, worthless, lost, pathetic, bitter, and lifeless~~" How do you think the author's usage of the slash-through affects the story? How would it be different without them?

NOTES

_____
_____
_____
_____
_____
_____
_____
_____
_____
_____
_____
_____
_____
_____
_____
_____
_____
_____
_____
_____
_____
_____
_____
_____
_____
_____
_____

_____

_____

_____

_____

_____

_____

_____

_____

_____

_____

_____

_____

_____

_____

_____

_____

_____

_____

_____

_____

_____

_____

_____

_____

_____

_____

_____

_____

_____

_____

_____

_____

_____

_____

_____

_____

_____

_____

_____

_____

_____

_____

_____

_____

_____

_____

_____

_____

_____

_____

_____

_____

_____

Mari Taylor